The
Importance
of Being
Ernest
the Earwig

For Huck, Zachary &
Elijah with love
N.N.

For Lilly, Bruno, Esme, Buddy,
Dylan & Ken with love
L.B.

Image of 'A Mad Tea-Party' by Sir John Tenniel from
The Nursery "Alice" by Lewis Carroll, published by Macmillan and Co 1889

Image of Cinderella from *Cinderella or the Little Glass Slipper*
published by McLoughlin Bros NY 1896

Image of 'Mole in the Wild Wood' by Helen Ward from
The Wind in the Willows by Kenneth Grahame, published by Templar Publishing 2000

Image of 'The birds were flown' by Gwynedd M. Hudson from
Peter Pan and Wendy by JM Barrie, published by
Hodder & Stoughton 1931

A TEMPLAR BOOK

First published in the UK in 2017 by Templar Publishing,
part of the Bonnier Publishing Group,
The Plaza, 535 King's Road, London, SW10 0SZ
www.templarco.co.uk
www.bonnierpublishing.com

Text copyright © 2017 by Nanette Newman
Illustration copyright © 2017 by Lindsay Branagh
Design copyright © 2017 by The Templar Company Limited

1 3 5 7 9 10 8 6 4 2

All rights reserved

ISBN 978-1-78370-636-5
Printed in China

The Importance of Being Ernest the Earwig

Written by

Nanette Newman

Illustrated by

Lindsay Branagh

t

templar publishing

It was one of those days when Ernest the Earwig was feeling gloomy.

"I've been thinking," he said to his friend, Edward, "if people take any notice of us earwigs, it's usually just to say 'Yuk' and flick us away. Why does nobody ever write stories about us?"

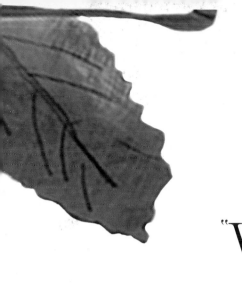

"What do you mean?" asked Edward.

"Well," said Ernest, "when have you ever
heard of a book about an earwig?
Like *The Mystery of the Phantom Earwig* or
The Adventures of Super Earwig.
Why are we always left out?"

Edward thought about this. "I don't
know," he said.

"Exactly," said Ernest. "Neither do I."

Then Ernest said, "I mean, take Nursery
Rhymes for instance. Why aren't we in any
of those? After all, why is the spider there
with Little Miss Muffet?"

"True," said Edward. "And it could have been:
'Little Bo Peep has lost her sheep and her earwig.'
Or 'Sing a song of sixpence, a pocket full of rye,
four and twenty earwigs baked in a pie.'"

"What about," said Edward, "'There was an old woman who lived in a shoe, she had so many earwigs she didn't know what to do?'"

"Perfect," said Ernest. "Oh, they write about birds and bees and butterflies and ladybirds— "

Edward interrupted. "'Ladybird, ladybird, fly away home, your house is on fire, your earwigs are gone.'"

A tear came into Ernest's eye. "Much better," he sighed. "Very moving."

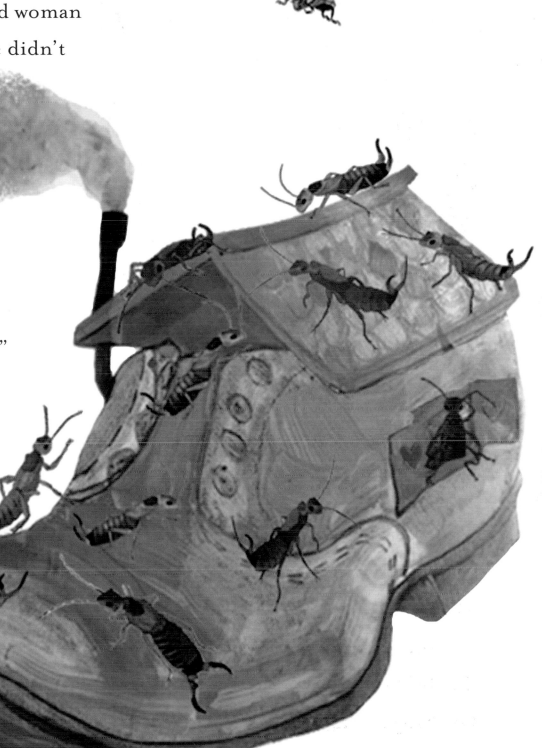

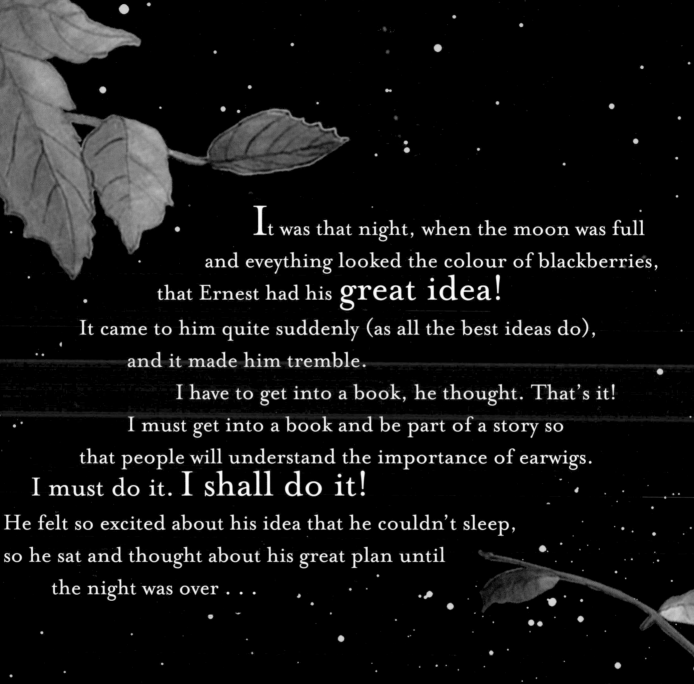

It was that night, when the moon was full
and eveything looked the colour of blackberries,
that Ernest had his great idea!

It came to him quite suddenly (as all the best ideas do),
and it made him tremble.

I have to get into a book, he thought. That's it!

I must get into a book and be part of a story so
that people will understand the importance of earwigs.
I must do it. I shall do it!

He felt so excited about his idea that he couldn't sleep,
so he sat and thought about his great plan until
the night was over . . .

Very early the next morning, Ernest hurried along to the bookshop. He waited for the shop to open, then he scurried inside. He saw a sign that said CHILDREN'S LITERATURE (Ernest knew that the word "literature" was just a fancy name for books).

This is it! Ernest said to himself. The moment I've been waiting for.

He ran up and down the shelves, reading the titles, until he came to *Alice in Wonderland.* Alice had so many exciting adventures, and such strange things happened to her — like falling down a rabbit hole and meeting all sorts of odd creatures.

He slid into the book . . . and to his delight, he found he had come in at the page where the Mad Hatter was having a Tea Party. There was the Dormouse, fast asleep, there was Alice and the March Hare . . . and, "No earwig," said Ernest. "Typical."
He sat on top of the Mad Hatter's hat so that Alice could see him.

Ever since Ernest was a tiny earwig

he had loved fairy tales,
so he scuttled along the shelves
until he found *Cinderella*.
He squeezed between the pages,
and there she was, sad and lonely . . .
He shouted as loud as an earwig
can shout (which isn't very loud):

"Don't worry, Cinders. You **shall** go to the ball!"

But Ernest couldn't wait for her to reply

because he had to get into the next book . . .

He then slithered in and out of the pages of his favourite story, *The Wind in the Willows*.

There was Mole, walking through the snow in the woods. He was frightened, so Ernest crawled onto his shoulder and whispered, "I'm here – I'm with you."

Then it was on to *Treasure Island.*
The excitement of sharing Jim's
adventure made Ernest's heart beat
faster — though he felt a bit sick on
the ship, and stayed well away from
Long John Silver's Parrot.

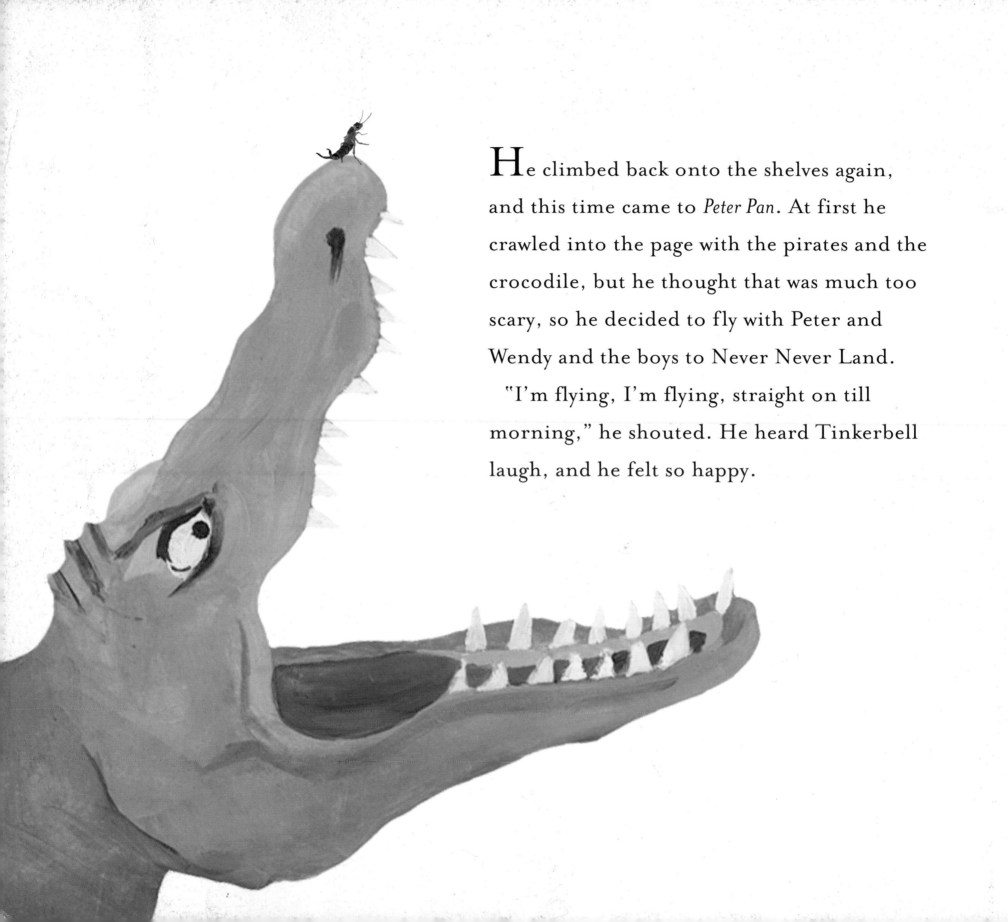

He climbed back onto the shelves again, and this time came to *Peter Pan*. At first he crawled into the page with the pirates and the crocodile, but he thought that was much too scary, so he decided to fly with Peter and Wendy and the boys to Never Never Land.

"I'm flying, I'm flying, straight on till morning," he shouted. He heard Tinkerbell laugh, and he felt so happy.

HEIDI
AND AN EARWIG

The Little Prince & the Earwig

SWALLOWS
AMAZONS
AND AN
EARWIG

Peter Pan
and an
earwig

THE
JUNGLE
BOOK
AND
THE
EARWIG

ALICE
IN
WONDERLAND
with an
earwig,

BLACK
BEAUTY
RUNS
WITH AN
EARWIG

THE
WIND
IN THE
WILLOWS

AND
THE
EARWIG

After his adventures Ernest was in need of a rest.

At last he knew what it was like to be in a book! The bookshop would be closing in a minute, so Ernest took one last look at the shelves and just for a moment it seemed as if every title included an earwig.

WHAT ERNEST DID NEXT

ILLUSTRATED

ERNEST THROUGH THE LOOKING GLASS

When he got home, he told Edward everything that had happened.

"Today," said Ernest, "I set out to prove that every creature — no matter how small, no matter how insignificant, no matter how unimportant they may seem — deserves the chance to be noticed!"

"I couldn't have said it better myself," said Edward.

"My dear friend," Ernest continued (with tears in his eyes), "today has made a new Earwig of me. I feel it is only proper that I should write a book about my experiences, my struggles, my achievements, for everyone to read."

"Oh definitely," said Edward. "I mean you must. What will you call it?"

Ernest thought . . . then said,

"The Importance of Being Ernest the Earwig."

Ernest cropped up in quite a few books after that. In fact if you turn the pages you will probably find he has managed to get into this one . . .